For Doug, my very own bear
B. B.

To Rowan
K. D.

Text copyright © 2008 by Bonny Becker
Illustrations copyright © 2008 by Kady MacDonald Denton

First paperback edition 2012

The Library of Congress has cataloged the hardcover edition as follows:

Becker, Bonny.
A visitor for Bear / Bonny Becker ; illustrated by Kady MacDonald Denton. — 1st ed.
p.   cm.
Summary: Bear's efforts to keep out visitors to his house are undermined by a very persistent mouse.
ISBN 978-0-7636-2807-9 (hardcover)
[1. Bears — Fiction. 2. Mice — Fiction. 3. Friendship — Fiction.]
I. Denton, Kady MacDonald, ill. II. Title.
PZ7.B3814Vis 2008
[E] — dc22   2006051850

ISBN 978-0-7636-4611-0 (paperback)

19 20 21 22 APS 19 18

Printed in Humen, Dongguan, China

This book was typeset in New Baskerville.
The illustrations were done in watercolor, ink, and gouache.

Candlewick Press
99 Dover Street
Somerville, Massachusetts 02144

visit us at www.candlewick.com

A Visitor for Bear

Bonny Becker

illustrated by
Kady MacDonald Denton

CANDLEWICK PRESS

No one ever came to Bear's house.
It had always been that way, and Bear
was quite sure he didn't like visitors.
He even had a sign.

One morning, Bear heard a tap, tap, tapping on his front door.

When he opened his door, there was a mouse, small and gray and bright-eyed.

"No visitors allowed," Bear said, pointing to the sign. "Go away."

He closed the door and went back to the business of making his breakfast.

He set out one cup and one spoon.

But when he opened the cupboard to get one bowl . . .

there was the mouse! Small and gray and bright-eyed.

"I told you to leave!" cried Bear.

"Perhaps we could have just a spot of tea?" said the mouse.

"Out!" commanded Bear.

"Most sorry," said the mouse. "I'll be going now."

Bear showed him to the door and shut it firmly.

Then he went back to the business of making his breakfast.

But when he opened the bread drawer for one slice of bread . . .

there was the mouse! Small and gray and bright-eyed.

"Unbelievable!" rumbled Bear.
"Away with you! Vamoose!"

"I do like a bit of cheese," said the mouse.

Bear pointed a rigid claw toward the door.

"Yes, then. Here I go," said the mouse. "Farewell."

And the mouse whisked out the door.

This time Bear shut the door very firmly and locked it tight.

He locked the windows, too, for good measure.

Then once again he went back to the business of making his breakfast.

But when he opened the fridge to get one egg . . .

there was the mouse!
(Small and gray and bright-eyed, of course.)

"BEGONE!"

roared Bear.

"A crackling fire?" ventured the mouse.

"This is impossible! Intolerable! Insufferable!" cried Bear, shaking with anger and disbelief.

"Terribly sorry," murmured the mouse. "Now you see me;
now you don't. I am gone."

And the mouse looked very sorry indeed while he waited
for Bear to unbolt the door and let him out again.

This time, before he went back to the business of making his breakfast, Bear shut the door very, VERY, VERY firmly, locked it,

boarded the windows shut,

stopped up the chimney,

and even plugged the drain in the bathtub.

Carefully, Bear set about the business of making his breakfast.
He opened the cupboard. No mouse. *Ahhhh.*

He opened the bread drawer. Nothing. *Whew!*

He opened the fridge. Mouse-free. *Yes, indeed!*

He lifted the lid to the teakettle.

There was the mouse!

Small and gray and, well, you know the rest.

Bear fell to the floor and wept.

"I give up," he blubbered. "You win.
I am undone."

"So sorry," said the mouse. "But perhaps if I could have just a bit of cheese and a cup of tea, and do you think we could unstopper the chimney and have a nice fire?"

Bear blew his nose with a loud honk.

"But then you must go," he sniffled. "No visitors allowed."

"You have my word," said the mouse.

Bear unshuttered and unboarded the windows,

unlocked the door,

unstoppered the chimney,

and unplugged the drain.

He brought out two plates of cheese and two teacups, and he made a crackling fire in the fireplace for two sets of toes.

The mouse warmed his feet and nibbled and sipped, and Bear did too.

They sat for a long while. The clock in Bear's house ticked loudly.

Bear cleared his throat.

The mouse looked most attentive. No one had ever been most attentive to Bear.

"The fire is nice," Bear announced.

"Lovely," said the mouse.

No one had ever said Bear's fires were lovely.

"I can do a headstand," said Bear.

"Very impressive!" exclaimed the mouse.

Bear told a joke. The mouse laughed heartily. No one had ever laughed at Bear's jokes before. Bear began to think of another joke.

The mouse set down his teacup. Bear quickly lifted the teapot.

"There's plenty more," he said.

"So sorry," said the mouse. "Most kind, but I must be on my way."

"Really, you needn't go," said Bear.

"I am off," said the mouse, springing up from his chair.

"Wait," cried Bear.

But the mouse stepped out the door.

"Toodle-oo," said the mouse.

"**Don't go!**" wailed Bear, throwing his body across the path.

"But I gave you my word," said the mouse, pointing at the "No Visitors" sign.

"Oh, that!" cried Bear, pulling down the sign and tearing it up.

"That's for salesmen. Not for friends."

"Not for friends?" asked the mouse, small and gray and bright-eyed.

Bear nodded. The mouse's bright eyes glowed brighter. Bear smiled.

"Do you like one lump or two?" said Bear, most politely.

"I like two," said the mouse. And Bear agreed.